chosen

Meghan Victoria

chosen

Radical Bookshop and Press
4838 Richard Road SW, Suite 300
Calgary, AB T3E 6L1

FIC029000 - Fiction, Short Stories

Chinook Blast Collection
Volume 1
February 1, 2021

Editors: Lexie Angelo
Cover Design: Lexie Angelo

ISBN-13: 978-1-990201-02-8

Printed in the United States

Typeset in Optima

*For the Corner Lot, and
scrappy writers everywhere.*

contents

PART 1

Something waits near the tree line.

For three nights Ava has felt its pull; the seduction of her thoughts, the torsion of her dreams. For three nights she has hovered near the window, uncertain. She presses her nose to the glass, her gaze on the wood that runs from the edge of her parent's property all the way to the river. She's ready.

Ava grabs her brother's ski-jacket from the closet and bundles it over the fleece of her housecoat. The snow looks hard and crusty and she keeps her slippers on; tough sealskin made for the elements. The moon is but a sliver as she steps outside, closing the door with a quiet click. Ava pauses and listens. The house is silent. She moves in the direction of the forest. Darkness swarms as she runs across the frozen lawn. A path well-worn, an escape from everyday life. She's learned to find peace in the unlit spaces of nature, but never silence, and the quiet of the wood prickles her arms.

A silhouette moves. Ava stumbles back. She clamps her lips shut against a scream. Clouds shift overhead, baring the moon. Pearly light sweeps the blackness, turning the shadow into a boy and scattering her thoughts of flight.

Everything about him is overwhelming. Too sharp, too pale. Too other.

Blond hair glistens against marble skin. Gray eyes appraise her. Flat. Dead. She sucks a breath but doesn't move.

"We need you," he says. "Come."

Her heart stutters. In fifteen years of her life, no one has ever needed her. Not in that tone. He turns, white wings trailing in the snow. She tries to catch her breath. To make sense of him. He disappears behind a tree and curiosity forces her feet to follow, nearly colliding with him as she rounds the bend. She realizes they are not alone, and heat floods her cheeks.

A woman kneels in the snow. Tattered clothes cling to her frail frame, pale skin bare against the night's chill. Her claw-like nails scratch symbols into the frozen earth.

"Baal, we haven't any time," says the woman. Her golden wings flare as her lilting voice steals across the clearing. An injured man lies beside her. His obsidian wings are open at awkward angles, unmoving. "Remor fades too quickly."

"Aislinn." The boy's voice holds a warning.

The woman looks up. They are strange names, ones Ava has never heard. Baal. Aislinn. Remor. Aislinn's violet eyes regard Ava, ancient and probing.

Ava takes a tentative step forward. "Is he — "

Aislinn's fingers are still against the snow. Another voice answers.

"Not yet," Baal says.

Ava takes another step. The man they call Remor comes into focus. His wings are shredded, his face marred by long gashes from forehead to chin.

"What happened to him?" Ava whispers.

"War," Aislinn says.

Baal makes a noise, guttural and deep.

Aislinn ignores him. "You have power, girl."

Ava bites back her doubt. She has never been special. Powerful.

"How?" she asks.

"Like this."

She flinches at the voice in her ear. Baal. He takes her chin between his long perfect fingers, tips her face and presses his lips against hers.

The world pauses. Her knees wobble. Fire unfurls in her chest, burning its way up her throat. Heat flows from her body to his. A kiss. Her first.

She pulls away, teetering. His strong hands steady her. Baal's eyes, once so flat and dead, are bright, alive. His skin glows, more silver than pallid after her touch.

"You understand?" he asks.

Something slithers in the pit of her stomach. She touches a finger to her lips. *We need you.*

"I can heal you?" she asks tentatively. She looks to Remor. "I can heal him?"

Baal nods.

"But … why me?"

"Because you have been chosen," Baal says, and there is foreboding in his words.

Ava kneels and brushes a midnight swatch of hair from Remor's savage face. She shakes as she draws cold air into her lungs. Slowly, slowly, she lowers her lips.

PART 2

The nights bleed into each other, turning days to weeks, weeks to months. Ava's life becomes a game of waiting for the winged strangers to return. And on the nights that they do, gasping for her gift of life, she pours herself into them. Healing them. Saving them.

Sometimes Baal comes alone, uninjured. He asks nothing of her and has not kissed her again since Remor lay dying. These are the nights that sustain her through the daylight hours.

"Do you fight in the war?" Ava asks on one such night, laying her head on Baal's shoulder, peering through stark branches at the midnight sky. A full moon stains the snow, painting the forest a palette of silver and gray.

"Yes." Baal's wingtip traces a frost-edged caress down her cheek.

"You're never injured." *You never need me.* She doesn't say the words out loud.

"I am the best." He caresses a thin thread of grey that spreads from her temple, the price she pays to keep them whole. "You give enough."

She tries to ignore the tingle that starts at her lips and spreads a fire that settles in her stomach. She pushes herself into his side, trying to ease the ache.

"What's it like? War?" she asks.

His feathered touch falls away. "Terrible."

A blazing arrow of light streaks across the sky.

"I wish I could fight with you," she whispers, watching it disappear into the velvety blackness. The moment stretches until it becomes stifling. She pulls away to look at him.

"Baal?"

"You should be wary of wishes," he says finally, his voice a ghost in the wind.

She exhales out frost-ridden air.

"I want to play a bigger part."

"We protect this world. In return, you protect us. It is enough."

His words are fierce.

"I'm not afraid," she says, tracing the patchwork of dirt and snow strewn across the forest floor. "I'm stronger than you think. This feeling … you feel it too. I'm meant to help."

His wings quiver, showering them in soft flakes from the tree branches above. "You're not like the others." His expression remains calm, cold, but his eyes blaze, burning into her.

Ava doesn't ask what he means by others. She doesn't want to know. He reaches for her, pulls her into his chest and buries his face in her hair. She closes her eyes and forces herself to breathe.

"Never change," he says fiercely, his breath hot against her skin.

Her lips part to offer the reassurance he seeks, but the words wilt against her tongue. She gives herself to his embrace and keeps her silence, unwilling to lie to him, unsure that this promise is one that she can keep.

*

Ava wakes abruptly. She peeks at the time, but it is still early. She has trained herself to wake at midnight, for they never come before the day has waned. Tonight, she is momentarily disoriented and wonders what has torn her from dreams of Baal's cutting gray eyes and cold lips.

A breeze drifts into the room. She doesn't remember leaving the window open. Not now, in the freezing depths of winter. Her teeth snag her lip, and she pulls her comforter tighter. She lies like this for a moment, listening. With a harsh exhale she pushes back the covers and swings her legs from her bed. Fear seems a silly emotion within the confines of her childhood bedroom. Her feet find her slippers and she pads across the room, hugging herself against the chill. Stretching, she pulls down the windowpane, wincing as it thuds closed. She peers through the glass, unable to shake the feeling of being watched. As she steps away, light gleams against the floor. Just below the ledge are three perfectly white feathers.

She whips around and squeaks at the sight of Baal sitting on the edge of her bed.

"Why are you here?" she whispers, hands clutching the thin material of her nightgown.

"To ensure that you remain whole," he says, his voice tightly controlled.

Ava scoots onto the bed. Baal's gaze doesn't stray from her face, but she draws her knees to her chest and wraps her arms around them. A tremble works its way through her body. Night after night they meet, always separated from reality by a haze of snow and shadow and wilderness. In the smallness of her bedroom, she is acutely aware of his maleness, of the repercussions attached to each action.

The bed shifts as Baal slides closer. One wing unfolds, slow and hesitant. Ava closes the space between them, leaning into the feathered embrace. Heat beats in her belly, fiery and insistent. She takes small, steady breaths before she speaks.

"What's wrong?" she asks.

"Remor is being … difficult."

Baal rarely speaks of his kin, and Ava stays silent. She waits, willing him to confide in her. When he says nothing, she gathers her resolve.

"Baal, will you stay the night?" she asks softly. "A storm is coming."

He studies her but his expression is unreadable.

She glances to the heavy flakes that coat the window. "You make me feel …" she pauses. Not safe, certainly. "Protected."

For a second she's afraid she's crossed some unspoken boundary. The expression, whatever it might have been, drains from Baal's face. He closes his gray eyes and remains still for several moments.

"Yes," he says finally.

He leans in and presses a kiss on her cheek, near the corner of her mouth. His hand, when it finds hers, is cold and solid. The flames in her stomach flicker in response.

PART 3

Tonight, the wind gusts from the west, luring ocean fog over the mountains and into the valley. Sitting in the forest, Ava tugs her threadbare blanket tighter against the chill. She hunkers close to the gnarled spruce trunks that surround her and waits, as she waits every night. A thud makes her flinch. She peers through the trees. Baal, only meters from her hiding place, his limbs twisted and broken.

She rushes towards him, her legs still stiff from kneeling in the snow. She blinks away the moisture gathering in the corners of her eyes.

"Baal," she whispers.

She cradles his head in her lap. With a fierce exhale she fastens her lips to his. She empties her soul into him, as she has been taught. Baal pushes her away, but her panic gives her strength. She feels the minute he accepts her sacrifice as ice seeps into her stomach. It claws through her chest and freezes her throat. Numbness follows, her grip loosens, and she finds herself drifting. She sways, unable to focus. She startles as strong hands grab and shake her. Her eyes flick open to Baal's furious stare. He stands and pulls her to her feet. Something is wrong.

"You idiot," he snarls. The sound of beating wings fills the air and, for the first time in the past months, fear steels across his features. He shoves her towards the forest.

"You must hide. Go!"

Ava lurches towards the tree line and falls to her knees. Her bare hands scramble against snow. She peels the discarded blanket from the ground and wraps it around her shoulders, biting the edge to stop her teeth from chattering.

Remor and Aislinn land soundlessly beside Baal.

"We'd thought you lost, brother," Remor says, his deep tenor reverberating through every crevice of the night.

"Hardly."

"It is good to see you well," Aislinn says. "We are too few, already."

Ava watches Aislinn's golden wings brush against the whiteness of Baal's, lingering with affection. She shivers at the memory of his white feathers against her skin. Remor keeps his distance, searching the trees. "We need the girl," he says.

Baal stills. "She is not ready."

"She? Or you? You asked for more time and I granted it. My patience begins to wear, Baal."

Baal glides towards him. "You may lead us into battle, *General*, but without me you have no soldiers."

They stand nearly nose to nose. Remor is broader and thicker, but Ava suspects Baal would best him should it come to a fight. She clutches herself, shivering. The world seems dimmer, somehow. She leans her head against a worn trunk and watches through half-veiled eyes.

"Enough." Aislinn lays a hand on Baal's arm. "We must not fight amongst ourselves."

Remor turns away with his shoulders tensed and wings flared. "It is what she desires. Or have you lost your touch?"

"She does not know for what she asks."

Ava flushes at his protective tone.

"Baal," Aislinn says quietly. "It must be done. We are holding this war at bay, but barely. There is still the prophecy."

"A child's tale." Baal flings open a wing. Snow catches and hurls into the distance. As he turns to Aislinn, his voice wavers, "There are other humans."

"You know there are not," she replies, and places a hand against Baal's cheek. The blanket falls from Ava's frozen fingers and she pulls herself to her feet. Her footsteps crunch, and they whirl to regard her.

"I'll do it," she says. "Whatever you need, I'll do it." Remor fixes his harsh gaze on her, but she doesn't flinch. Baal refuses to meet her eye.

"Bravery, how refreshing." Remor flexes his black wings to the sky. "See that it is done. Come, Aislinn."

Ava blinks. A cluster of gold and black feathers darken the snow. Remor and Aslinn are gone. Baal sweeps his wing, scattering the reminders of his kin. Ava creeps toward him.

"Baal, what's happening? Why are you so angry?"

"You should run." His voice is flat, resigned.

"I'm not afraid."

"You should be." His eyes are rimmed scarlet, the gray of his iris' turned black.

She reaches for him and he hesitates before drawing her into his arms. Over the clearing there is a brooding silence, a hush that confines the world to the steady rise and soft surrender of every breath.

"I don't understand," Ava whispers against Baal's chest.

He steps from their embrace, silver hair catching a swatch of moonlight as he begins to pace. "We ruled this world, once. The skies, the waters — even the very air belonged to us. But the coming of man tipped the balance and released a darkness that we could not contain."

"The war," she whispers.

He nods. "It falls to us to protect this world from the demons your kind have unleashed."

"Unleashed how?"

"Deceit. Murder. Small unkindnesses. There was a balance once, but the world has changed, and the demons have become too many. And we, too few."

Ava stretches out a hand, but Baal turns away.

"What does this have to do with me? With you?" she asks.

Baal's wings trace downy patterns in the snow as they trail behind him. Ava shifts her weight from foot to foot, trying to force feeling into her frozen limbs.

"My kind are a dying breed," Baal says. "Soon, there will not be enough of us left to fight. It is my duty to ensure that does not happen. My duty to recruit humans and turn them."

"Turn them into what?"

"Monsters."

The word lingers.

Ava raises a trembling hand and tucks a stray strand of dark hair behind her ear. She glances to the small, flickering porch light of her house in the distance.

"Remor calls them warriors but they are the damned." Bitterness clouds Baal's voice. "Most humans cannot survive it. Only the purest, the ones who can heal us. Only they can be turned."

20

"Is this what you plan to do to me? Turn me into a monster?"

Baal turns to face her but doesn't meet her gaze. "There is a prophecy to end the evil. It says that one human will be turned and will reject the darkness. One human will become like us and lead us to salvation."

"And you think I am that human?" Her question trembles in the cold night air.

"It's possible."

"And if I'm not? What exactly does it mean to turn a person into a monster?"

He meets her gaze now, his gray eyes unfathomable. "You will cease to be Ava. You will become slave to your instincts, to your hunger, to war. Deadly to our enemies. A violent, wretched thing."

"You're trying to scare me away," she says.

"You should be scared." His voice is hard.

"I'm not." It's a lie, but she grabs his hand and pulls him close. "Why explain this to me? Why not just change me and be done with it?"

He hesitates and rubs his thumb against her knuckles. "Because you must choose. I cannot force this upon you."

Sound slips past her lips. A laugh. A sob. "I love you."

Gently, he pulls his hand from her grip. "We are created so that humans fall in love with us. It is how we survive and how we fulfill our duty. Your love will protect you no more than any other mortal."

She flinches, realizing others have loved him. They have given themselves to him, each one thinking they might be the girl in the prophecy, and each one of them failing.

"Do you love me?" she asks, watching him closely.

He stiffens. "Love is a tool. A weapon."

She studies his face in the liquid moonlight. "Maybe you're right," she says softly. "But love is a human weapon. Mine, not yours." She takes his hand once more, threading her fingers with his. "What we have is different. *I* am different. You said it yourself."

His wings fold around her. "Don't do this, Ava. *Please.*"

The sound of her name on his lips sparks embers deep in her lungs, burning oxygen, leaving her breathless.

She manages a whisper. "I trust you."

"Don't."

"If I choose this, can you resist? Just walk away?"

She thinks she can hear the hammering of his heart.

"I am bound to honor your choice," he says finally, so quietly she has to strain to catch the words.

It is enough.

This time, the kiss is hers to initiate. She stands on her tiptoes, presses her lips to his. It begins as everything she has been waiting for, hungry and fierce. But then it mutates, desperate and apologetic, sucking at her soul as it swallows light, replacing it with darkness. She tries to scream, but that, too, is swallowed. Her body convulses and begin to change. She struggles and tries to pull free. Panic bubbles as her back sears with pain. Her skin splits. Her bones grind and break. Her face is wet, her mind frantic, howling, shrieking at everything to stop.

And then, quiet.

Baal untangles himself. He lays the body of the creature that is no longer Ava on the ground. His face is streaked with tears and blood, though whose, it is not clear. The body twitches. Black wings unfurl, ragged and bat like. A hoarse rasping escapes. One clawed hand heaves the body into a crouch. Crimson eyes open.

"Come," Baal says, his voice flat and dead. "War awaits."

ACKNOWLEDGEMENTS

Eternal gratitude goes to the Corner Lot Authors: Leesa Iverson, Olyn Ozbick, Gail Lowe, Vivian Heather, and Lisa Weir. You make me a better writer, a better person, and a better friend. Sarah L. Johnson helped coax this fledging idea into something with teeth and heart. Without you and your relentless encouragement, this story wouldn't exist. Sarah, Jaclyn, Alex, Nick, Natalie and Drew – thank you for countless hours of critique, wine and laughter.

A huge thank you to the Alexandra Writers' Centre Society and its incredible instructors, most notably Theanna Bischoff, Rosemary Nixon, and Robin van Eck. You taught me the difference between show versus tell, that thick skin is necessary in the business of writing, and that in the end, nothing ventured, nothing gained.

Finally, to my wonderful family: Danny, Melissa, Clint, Jack, Pat, Dick, Jenn, Brad, Alex, April, Mom and Dad. Your encouragement means the world to me.

ABOUT THE AUTHOR

Meghan grew up in the frozen wilds of Labrador, listening to too much symphonic metal and writing really bad poetry. She eventually made her way to Calgary, Alberta, where she found a writing community that turned into family. Meghan's short fiction has been featured by Coffin Hop Press, the Antigonish Review, and various other magazines and anthologies. She teaches creative writing at the Alexandra Writers' Centre Society and spent two years as part of the Banff Centre's Writing Self-Residency Program. When not crafting new worlds or crying over the editing process, you can find Meghan hiking across far-flung continents, teaching yoga, and still writing really bad poetry.

SPECIAL THANKS

Chinook Blast Festival

The City of Calgary

Tourism Calgary

Calgary Municipal Land Corporation

Calgary Arts Development

Calgary Public Library

IngramSpark